10/23/02

To my big sister,
Beth Le Doux, with love

—F. H.

For Rajan Troll

—V. R.

Henry Holt and Company, LLC
Publishers since 1866
115 West 18th Street, New York, New York 10011

Library of Congress Cataloging-in-Publication Data
Hill, Frances. The bug cemetery / by Frances Hill; illustrated by Vera Rosenberry.
Summary: Neighborhood children imaginatively stage funerals for dead bugs,
but they experience real sadness following the death of a pet.
[1. Death—Fiction. 2. Grief—Fiction. 3. Loss—Fiction.]
I. Rosenberry, Vera, ill. II. Title. PZ7.H5518 Bu 2001 [E]—dc21 00-57532
ISBN 0-8050-6370-6 / First Edition—2002 / Designed by Donna Mark
Printed in the United States of America on acid-free paper. ∞
1 3 5 7 9 10 8 6 4 2

The artist used gouache on Lanaquarelle paper
to create the illustrations for this book.

The Bug Cemetery

BY Frances Hill

ILLUSTRATED BY Vera Rosenberry

HENRY HOLT AND COMPANY

NEW YORK

When I found a dead ladybug one day, my sister, Wilma, buried it for me. She painted a rock to use as a tombstone.

I picked flowers from the garden and covered the mound of dirt.

Then Wilma gave a moving speech about the dead
ladybug's life while I pretended to cry for it.

Billy, who lives next door, found a dead fly.

That afternoon we had another bug funeral. This one
was better, with two people pretending to cry.

Wilma started charging a dime to bury someone's dead bug. Billy opened a lemonade stand for thirsty mourners. Business was booming. Soon we had a bug cemetery in our backyard.

Our father thought we should dig up the bug
cemetery and plant a flower garden in its place.

But our mother didn't agree. She said creating
our cemetery showed initiative.

So we got to keep the cemetery. I was glad.
I thought funerals were fun.

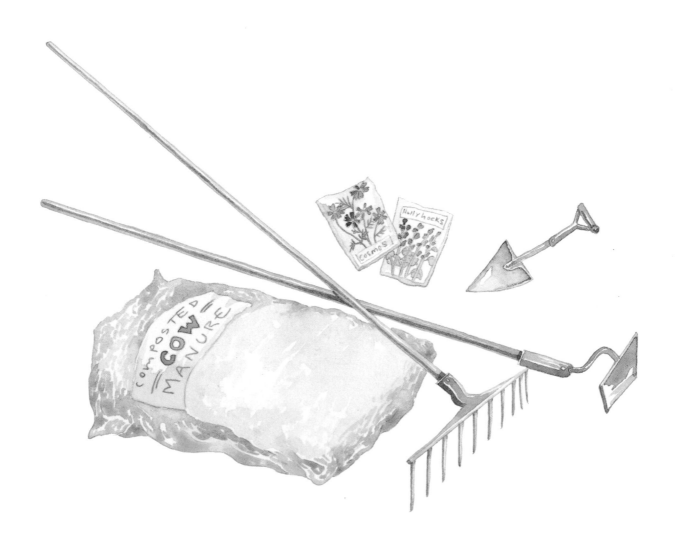

Then Billy's cat, Buster, was accidentally hit by a car.

Buster died.

Billy wanted to bury Buster in the bug cemetery.
"Buster likes to chase bugs," he said. "He'll be
happy here."

So we buried Buster in the bug cemetery. I cried real
tears at the funeral. Billy did too. Even Wilma cried.

Funerals aren't any fun when they're for someone you love.

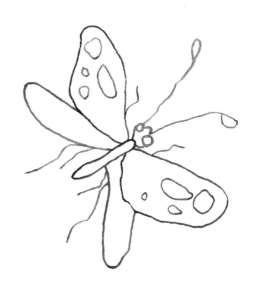

Wilma painted a tombstone for Buster's grave
and covered it with butterflies. Butterflies were
Buster's favorite bug to chase.

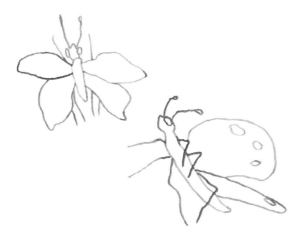

No one felt like coming to funerals anymore, so we stopped burying bugs in the bug cemetery. We helped our father plant a garden around Buster's grave.

Now the bug cemetery is full of flowers that butterflies like.

We call it Buster's Garden.

And Billy has a new kitten. He named him Buster the Second. I saw the kitten today in Buster's Garden. He was chasing a butterfly.